SELLING HER AGE GAP

Reverse Harem Mafia

Leandra Camilli

ISBN: 9798437843543
Imprint: Independently published

1st edition

Cover design by: Leandra Camilli

CONTENTS

CHAPTER 1

Being rich didn't mean that I could do anything I wanted. In fact, it was the opposite. When I learned that my father wanted to marry me to a stranger, I was furious. So furious that he ended up putting me on this ship, which was headed toward Europe. He didn't even tell me what country it was. Just that I needed to keep my head low and pretend that nothing was happening.

But that was difficult to do especially when everything that could go wrong was. I had just walked into my room on the ship when I realized that something in it was missing. It was something important to me. It was given to me by my grandmother when she was still alive.

It was a comb. She gave it to me for my 13th birthday and I still remembered it fondly. So much so that I didn't throw it away when it started to break. I kept it with me, always using it when I needed to comb my hair.

I looked around everywhere in the room, but I didn't find the comb.

Was there a suspect? There was and I didn't want to think about it. I didn't want to admit that she was such an asshole that she was doing this to me.

Nevertheless, I jumped out of the room before spinning to the right. Putting one foot forward, I started to march toward her room. I could feel the ship swaying left and right on the ocean. It was making me a little dizzy, but it was nothing that was going to impede me from doing the right thing.

My blood was boiling. I had never felt so angry before in my life.

A few seconds later, I stopped in front of the door to her room. I wasted no time before rapping on it. If she was still in there, then she was going to come out and give me my comb back. There was no other way that this could play out.

I wasn't going to forgive her for this, though.

And just when I thought I heard footsteps coming from the other side of the door, I heard someone coming my way from the left. I turned to see who it was, because I was that curious and also because I had the attention span of a goldfish, when I then bumped against him.

My eyes went up as I realized that it was a huge man that just bumped into me. He was so huge that he made me feel incredibly small, even though I wasn't a small girl. He had something in his hand, which appeared to be a book.

The sweat on his forehead showed me that he was in a hurry. To go where, I didn't know, but I already wanted to find out. He regarded me with a lack of sympathy, as if he couldn't care less about me. I should be angry that that was his reaction, but I felt the opposite. It was the first time that I was in the presence of a man who didn't want to fall to his knees right away, and then there was a flash of something in his eyes which showed me that he thought I was hot.

I felt some heat rising to my cheeks. He was handsome and it flattered me that he thought that way about me. My eyes went down slowly, taking in the curves and the lines of his body. They were perfect, not too harsh, and not too round, either. And even though he wore a suit, I could tell that his body was well-built.

The man was built like a tank was what I was trying to say.

He still had some beard to be made, but I didn't think that he was going to do anything about it anytime soon. He liked the little scruff on his face, I could tell. I could also tell that it had some gray hairs, which was puzzling. He looked a little older than me, but not by much more.

It certainly made him look sexier, I thought.

It was like time was frozen around me and all I could see were his eyes on me. It was almost as if they were burning through my soul and reading everything I was thinking. His eyes were icy blue, perfect as they were. They had a hint of warmth in them, but for the most part, they were freezing cold. So much so that I found it difficult to imagine that he could feel empathy for anyone.

I could see his Adam's apple bobbing up and down, showing me that he was a little nervous, even though he was hiding that fact well. One could look at him and think that I was going crazy about it, that someone like him could never feel nervousness, but that wasn't what I was seeing right now.

His body had such a presence that I didn't just feel small before him, but also incredibly warm, especially down there. My pussy was hotter and wetter than when I bumped against him. The last thing I thought could happen now was that I was going to stumble on someone so sexy and hot, whose harsh facial features were a sight to behold.

I noticed that he dropped the book that he was taking with him. I crouched, reaching out with my hand as I grabbed it. I slowly stood up as my eyes scanned his body from bottom to top, taking in the fact that his feet were enormous. For a brief moment, my mind recollected that saying that 'big feet meant having a big cock', but I quickly brushed it off.

It was just a joke and a silly one at that.

I lifted my hand that was holding the book. "Here. I'm so sorry I ended up bumping against you. It wasn't my intention," I said, trying to make it so my voice didn't sound too weak, even though doing that was almost impossible in the presence of such an imposing man.

"It was nothing. I know that it wasn't your intention. Not to mention that I should have paid better attention to where I was going, anyway."

When he spoke, I noticed that his accent was different, although I couldn't put my finger on where it came from. It was certainly from a European country, though.

And the door behind me opened just when I remembered that I came here for something else. *Sofia, that bitch.* She was going to pay for stealing my comb.

My eyes glared at her when I realized that she was looking at me with those same cynical eyes. She was with the elbow of her arm propped against the doorway, resting her head on her hand. She didn't have her shirt on, which was a sin in on itself. I couldn't even stand looking for more than a fraction of a second at her.

Seeing that, I turned my head quickly the other way, saying, "Just give me my comb back. It's what I came here for."

"Really?" She asked, her eyes immediately going up and down, I noticed even though I wasn't looking at her face anymore. She was checking out the man that was right behind me and whose name I didn't even bother to ask. My mind was such a whirlwind of thoughts that that didn't even cross my mind. "Because I thought you were trying to hit on Leonardo."

Leonardo? I knew his name had to be different from what I was used to, but I didn't think that it was Italian. I slowly reopened my eyes, looking at his face and seeing something different. I was seeing the face of a man who was probably heading back to his home country. I supposed that the ship was heading to Italy, then.

Nevertheless, I had to brush that thought out of my mind right away. It served me no purpose.

I turned to the right slowly when I felt that something was in the corner of my vision. It was the comb that was so dear to me. Sofia was holding it in her hand, I noticed as I also took note of the fact that she was chewing gum. Gosh. Could she be any more disgusting? I asked myself, realizing that that question was pointless.

I reached out with my hand, grabbing the comb.

Leonardo grabbed the book from my hand, his hand cupping mine. It was at that moment that I realized that his hand was big and heavy. So much so that it made my hand feel smaller than normal.

He was so dominating, I could tell. I couldn't help but wonder what he was like in bed, not that I was thinking we had a chance of getting laid, though.

It wasn't going to happen and that was something I needed to keep in mind.

It wasn't going to happen and that was something I needed to keep in mind.

CHAPTER 2

"You are telling me you don't believe in love at all?" He asked, holding me close to his body. It was a strong, built-like-a-tank body. His eyes were on me as we kept ourselves afloat in the water. His legs swung gently under it, trying to teach me how to do it. I didn't know how to swim, which was something that deeply ashamed me. Well, now I was finally doing something about that.

"I don't," I replied, my eyes diverting downward and checking out his lips. They were rosy, perfect as they were. He had a slight overbite, which was excitably sexy. Just looking at his lips right now, I wanted to kiss him, even though I shouldn't.

And one of the reasons for that was that he was the one my father wanted to marry me with. And being with him, him being my swimming lessons teacher, wasn't something that I thought I would end up stumbling on while I was on the ship.

His body was perfect, with almost no body fat. I could feel his abs pressing against my belly, making me want to move my hand where they were and to slide it over their curves, feeling every ridge and crevice.

Given the look in his eyes, I could tell that he thought the same. He was naughty and I wasn't going to deny that.

Screams, laughs, chatters, and splashes of water around me told me that I wasn't alone, which was a good thing. I didn't know what would be happening right now if we weren't. If we were alone, I was pretty sure that he would take advantage of me, which wasn't something I wanted.

One of the things I didn't even want to think about right now was the fact that he was hard. I could feel his hard-on pressing against my pussy through my bikini. And it was big. His package was massive, bigger than anything I thought I knew. He was probably even bigger than most guys on porn movies.

"That's a shame. I was wondering if I could win your heart over," he teased, his lips dangerously close to touching against mine. I studied his eyes and I wondered if he was thinking the same thing. I didn't want to do it, but the fact was that I had never kissed anyone and here I had this beefcake almost kissing me. I was almost wondering if I shouldn't just do it. "I thought you were going to love me."

The aroma coming out of his mouth was minty. It went into my lungs, impregnating it with its smell. I could do nothing against it, and it was melting my body. Even though I struggled against his embrace, it was a weak attempt.

I chuckled. Gervasio could be quite the joker when he wanted to.

And yet, that was nothing more than just one thing that I quickly brushed off.

I wrapped my arms around his shoulders, pressing more tightly against his body. My boobs were pressing against his chest, and he loved that. The look in his eyes was telling of that. It wasn't lying to me about that.

He opened a big, bright smile, saying, "Wow there, I didn't think you were going to do that," and then he lowered his arms around my body, following the curves of it, eventually settling his hands on my asscheeks. He cupped both of them with them, making me emit a moan.

"Gosh, that's so good," I murmured into his ear, betraying the fact that I didn't want to fall in love with him. I shouldn't. He was going to do unspeakable things to me if I did.

Nevertheless, his body was just so warm right now and extremely inviting, and I could do nothing against that. Then, as if to tease me even more than he already was, he slipped one of his fingers under my bikini, locking his eyes with me one more time.

I had to admit it. It was difficult to read what he was thinking.

"Do you want me to go on?" He murmured into my ear, widening his smile. What a jerk. I knew that nobody was going to find out. We were in the swimming pool on the ship and the water covered part of our bodies, but Gervasio was still taking a huge risk. If anyone dived underwater, they could notice it. And if that happened, I would be so flustered I wouldn't know what to say.

"Yes…" I responded and it was the only thing I could say. My pussy was so wet and it wasn't just because of the water. My orgasmic juices were leaking out, and Gervasio was aware of that. So much so that I was pretty sure that, regardless of my answer, he would have gone on.

"That's the answer I expected from you and it's the right one, too," he continued. His finger moved left and right around my asscheeks and then he glided it toward my asshole. I wanted him to go further down where my pussy was, but he was always such a tease. Gervasio wasn't going to do everything I wanted.

Moments later, his finger was where he wanted it to be. On my asshole, prodding it. He knew how to brush his finger in all the right directions and when to use all the right speeds. My body started to shake, my eyes closing slightly.

Gervasio was turning me on in front of everyone while he still pretended that he was just teaching me how to swim.

He dipped his head, putting it close to mine. Everything was even warmer around me than it was moments ago.

"People are going to find out," I tried to warn, but the widening of his smile on his face told me that he didn't care. Gervasio was like that.

"And, what about it?" He hissed, his lips pecking my lips all of a sudden.

It happened so suddenly that I didn't know what to do. I just bulged my eyes out before shooting him the following question, "What the hell was that?"

He slipped his finger inside my asshole, making me moan. "Oh, baby. You know exactly why I am doing this. You think I'm a monster, that I kill people for sport, but that isn't the case. You hate me so much and yet you melt in my arms like this."

His dick was raging in his underwear, and I couldn't help but feel that I should do something about that. The only problem was that I didn't even know what to do. Even though we were having such a sexy moment together, I had no experience with what was happening.

And that lack of experience was showing right now.

"Maybe I should just kill you right now," I threatened, moving around with him in the water. His finger was still inside my rectum and I didn't think he was going to take it out of there anytime soon. Gervasio was tormenting me right now and he knew he was doing that.

"You won't. I'm going to make you come so hard right now that you are going to be questioning if you should continue hating me."

I bulged my eyes out one more time. I knew that what he just promised was the truth, or at least it was going to be so in a matter of seconds. I bit my bottom lip hard because I didn't want anyone around us to hear it. If they did, they wouldn't just kick me out of the swimming pool area, but also out of the ship.

I knew that my father was powerful and influential, but he wouldn't stand against them for me.

"Please, stop..." I begged him, but I didn't think he was going to listen to me. I was so right about that that he continued to rub and spin his finger inside my rectum, driving me crazy. "Everyone is going to hear us."

"Oh, let them hear everything. It's not like they can do anything about it, anyway."

I curled up the side of my lips, hating the fact that Gervasio barely even listened to what I murmured. What a jerk, and yet he was a jerk that I was beginning to fall in love with. Even though I hated him as a person, he was going to be the one to take my virginity. There was no denying that.

Moments later, when I started to hump against his junk and he bumped up the pace with which his finger was destroying my asshole, I finally came. My body started to rock and shake, and it was only thanks to the fact that his arms were keeping me locked with him that nobody around us noticed anything.

I could almost close my eyes and fall asleep, but I didn't. Gervasio was impeding me from doing that.

CHAPTER 3

Curled up in the bedsheets, all I could feel was the gentle sway of the ship as it continued to cruise the ocean. I was thinking back to what happened that afternoon when I was with Gervasio. His room was on the other side of the ship.

I... I was pretty sure that tonight he was going to come for me.

I was so sure about that that I kept the door open. It was unlocked and he could just open it. I had nothing more than my bra and my pair of panties on. If he found me in the condition that I was in, he would feel ashamed of me.

I twisted gently under the bedsheets when I started to hear footsteps coming in my direction. They were like gunshots sounding in the hallway, the person that owned them certain that he was coming where I was.

The room where I was on the bed was dark and everything around me was quiet. I twisted my body in the bedsheets one more time, my pussy hot and wet. Gervasio gave me that amazing orgasm while he was teaching me how to swim, but it wasn't enough. I wanted him to take my virginity. I wanted him to come inside of me.

All these years with my family keeping me locked up in my room, allowed only to venture outside some days so that I could walk around in the property, turned me into a slut. So much so that the only thing I could think about was sex.

I couldn't help but wonder just how big his slab of meat was, and it looked like I was going to find out the answer to that soon. A man just put his hand against the door, opening it. I heard it creaking, but it didn't bother me. Even though the ship was dead silent, nobody was going to pay any attention to what was happening in my room.

I curled up when I heard him closing the door. I was pretty sure that it was Gervasio. It had to be. He was the only one that knew I was in this room on the ship.

"Gervasio?" I asked, wondering if he was going to answer me. But when he didn't, I wasn't surprised. I knew he wasn't going to answer my question. So much so that when he sat down on the bed, I knew he wasn't going to say anything, which he didn't. "Please say something," I still pleaded.

He chuckled. My eyes were open, but I could only make out the silhouette of his body. He didn't have any clothes on. I could see the curves of his muscles under the dimmed light coming from the moon and through the small window of the room.

A moment later, he settled his hand on my leg, keeping it there for what felt like minutes. I wondered if he was going to do anything else, and I wasn't surprised when I felt his hand gliding up. He was looking for my ass, and maybe even for my cunt, and he was going to stop at nothing.

I tried to move my leg, but then he clasped his hand around it, stopping it.

"Why?" I asked, even though I knew he wasn't going to answer me. "Why are you such a jerk?"

Once again, Gervasio said nothing. He didn't have to. When he grabbed my leg, I knew that he said he didn't want me to move it. He wanted me paralyzed and frozen just like I was, as if I was a painting.

His hand was heavy and calloused. It was the first time that I was feeling a man's hand that was like that.

Gervasio knew who he was and the power that he commanded over me. In light of that, I wasn't surprised, not even in the slightest, when his hand went to where my pussy was. He snuck one of his fingers under my pair of panties, touching my clit.

He started to rub it over and over as the seconds passed, and they were passing dangerously slowly. I moaned louder than ever before, not knowing for how much longer I could stand his wrath.

I just wanted to hear his voice one more time and I knew that he wasn't going to say anything, which was such a dangerous torment.

Then, he stopped making circular movements with his finger. When he wasn't rubbing it anymore, I felt that I could finally breathe again. And breathe I did, but only for a couple seconds. If I thought that just one of his fingers was enough to drive me crazy, I knew that a second one was going to be even more excruciating.

He leaned over, his body on top of me. I could better make out what the curves of his muscles were like, finally bringing enough strength to put my arms around his body. My fingers pressing against the hardness of his muscles, I just wanted him inside of me. His fingers were inside of me that time when we were swimming, but I craved something more.

"What are you doing? You're taking your time and that's pissing me off," I hissed, knowing that he wasn't going to take that well. And he didn't. He increased the speed with which his finger was rubbing my clit and then stopped what he was doing.

He started to play with my pussy folds, gently sliding his fingers against them. As he continued to do that, I roamed my hands around his body, making sure that I wasn't hurting him with my nails.

He huffed slightly and then kissed my shoulder, making his way upward. I parted my lips moments before he kissed me. We started to make out and his tongue immediately went inside my mouth. We then shared a short tongue battle, and it was so brief that I didn't even realize it was over when it already was.

His fingers lingered against mine when he grabbed my hand. His hand was so big that mine felt incredibly tiny, and I knew that any ounce of resistance I still had against him just crumbled.

When he pulled his head back slightly, a line of drool still connected our lips.

And in the meantime, I slid my hand downward, finding his ass. For a moment, I thought that his asscheeks were slightly different from what I was used to, but I didn't give that thought much importance. I was just happy that I could bathe in the warmth of his body, feeling the softness of his asscheeks.

And then, I did something I thought I wasn't going to. I snuck my hand under his pair of boxer briefs, which was the only piece of clothing he wore. I thought that he wore nothing when he stepped inside the room.

I moved it around his waist before finding what I was seeking. It was his hard, raging cock. The moment I felt it, I flinched, but only for a fraction of a second.

Even though I couldn't make out his face in the darkness, I knew that he just smiled.

Then, he lowered his head as he planted his lips against my neck. I arched my back, and then I responded to that by wrapping my fingers around his cock. It was so big that my hand felt tiny again, which was something I realized was a constant between us.

Gervasio still played with my pussy folds and it appeared that he wasn't going to stop doing that anytime soon. As the seconds ticked by, I realized that I was on the verge of orgasming again.

"You are such a jerk and I'm going to keep saying that until you finally say something back," I muttered, each word hurting me.

Just like all the other times, as if he was doing everything in his power to hide something, he kept his lips sealed.

I started to pump his shaft over and over, and it didn't get any harder than it already was. He was ready to penetrate me, to breach me with his man tool, and I couldn't wait for that any longer.

Then, he retreated his hand and grabbed my hand – the one that was grabbing his cock. He made me pull it back, which I did even though I didn't want to.

For a fraction of a second, I wondered what was going to ensue, and then I realized what his endgame was. I widened my eyes at that same moment. It surprised me. It more than did that, in fact. It shocked me and I could do nothing about it.

"What are you going to do now?" I asked the same moment that he tore off my pair of panties without warning. One moment it was protecting my pussy against him and the next it was nowhere to be seen.

And when he spoke, I just realized that he wasn't Gervasio.

CHAPTER 4

In fact, he was someone else entirely. He was the same man whose name I didn't even ask when I bumped into him when we were in the hallway. If my eyes were already wide before, now they were as if they were going to jump out of my head.

I lunged away from him, but then he just grabbed my legs all of a sudden. His grip was strong and determined. Even through the darkness in the room, his eyes glared at me.

"You aren't going anywhere, little princess," he said and his voice was the same that I had heard at that time. I should be trying to kick him, but I couldn't. His grip was just so strong that I couldn't even move my legs an inch.

"You are hurting me," I said, noticing that I just lost that rising feeling of an orgasm that was going to wash over me. If this man was thinking that the way he just popped up in my room was going to make me fall in love with him too, then he had something coming.

"What's your name? So that I can report you to the police."

He straightened his back slowly, regarding me with his eyes. For a moment, I thought he wasn't going to say anything, but then he replied, "It's Leonardo. You should already know that about me. Do you have dementia or something like that?"

I slapped at his shoulder, feeling furious at what he just insinuated. "Of course not. I'm just angry at what you did. I was expecting someone else."

Sofia did tell me his name before. I must've forgotten it for a brief moment.

I could still feel the pressure where his fingers were. It was like they were still there. The way he just showed up in my room unannounced would forever remain in my mind and, at the start, it was a huge turnoff, but now I couldn't stop thinking about it. And in return, my pussy was beginning to get hotter, too.

"Who were you expecting? That loser that wants to be your husband?" He growled, making me wonder if they had some kind of history between them that I wasn't aware of. Nevertheless, I made no questions about that. I didn't want to involve myself with something I didn't have anything to do with, at least not on the surface.

And after a moment of silence, he asked, "Did you like what I was doing?"

I bit my bottom lip. I didn't want to admit to this asshole that he was right about that, but I also felt offended by the way he just showed up in my room.

When he noticed my reaction, he said, "I'm really sorry about the way I just showed up here. It won't happen again, I promise."

I studied his face for a couple of seconds, trying to find out if he was telling the truth or not. When I realized that that was nothing more than a fruitless endeavor, I just shook my head.

"I'm not going to say anything," I said, my voice low and throaty. I wasn't going to admit to this jerk that he was right about anything.

In light of that, I crossed my arms over my chest, pouting.

He leaned over slightly, being so close to me that I could feel his minty breath. It was intoxicating and it was also making it very hard for me not to keep looking at him.

"I like it when girls like you make it harder for me. There's nothing like beating a challenge."

"Fuck you!"

"No," he said, widening his smirk, "I'm going to fuck you."

The moment he said that, I expected that he was going to lunge at me, but he didn't. He stayed where he was, his eyes confident and staring at me.

It was like he was reeling me in with his stare alone. Fighting against his wrath was pointless. He wanted me and I craved him. Gervasio made me feel so good, but he wasn't here and, as time passed, I began to think that he wasn't going to show up.

"He isn't here. I'm going to do so much more to you than what he can," Leonardo promised, grabbing my legs again, but this time he was much more gentle. It was like his hands were made of silk. Whatever strength I had before just melted and there was nothing I could do about that.

"Can you promise me one more thing?" I asked, my voice sounding like I just begged.

Hearing that, he slid his hands further up until they were almost touching my pussy. I thought he was going to do it, that he was going to begin tormenting my cunt with his fingers again, but it was obvious that he had other plans in mind.

"Whatever you wish, my princess," he purred, kissing my right leg once and then twice in a row. His lips were just so warm and wet, which was exactly the way I wanted them to be.

"Can you do it slowly?"

For a moment, the question hung in the air and I had no idea if he was even going to answer it. When I was already growing nervous and frustrated at his lack of response, he replied, "Of course. I'm going to do it much better than Gervasio did. It will be slow and, sometimes, even painful, but things will be better. I'm going to do it so much better than he did that you will think at least five times before getting married to him."

Hearing that gave me the relief that I needed. I then closed my eyes, tilted my head backward, and widened the gap between my legs.

Leonardo broadened his smile, kissing my legs again, and this time the kiss was much slower than the first one – and also the second one. It was as if his lips melted my skin. The longer that they were in contact with it, the stronger I felt that I was going to pass out.

My breathing quickened, sweat started to come out of my pores, and I gripped the bed sheets tightly. He was relentless, making his way up as he kissed me from the lower part of my legs to where my cunt was.

But then, Leonardo stopped. I thought that he was going to quickly resume what he was doing, but then I realized that he froze up. I opened my eyes again as I realized that he was still smiling.

"What? Thinking that I was just going to stop like this and leave you hating me?" He murmured, moving so that his head was right between my legs and no more than a couple of inches from my pussy.

He thrust his tongue out, flicking it over my clit. Each flick sent shockwaves of pleasure through my whole body, making it shake and rock. I gripped the bedsheets so tightly I thought I was going to tear them. My vision started to blacken and I even thought I was going to pass out for sure this time, but I didn't.

I was still right where I was, on the bed, my lungs begging for air.

"That was delicious, wasn't it?" He asked, lowering his hands so that he was cupping the region just under my ass cheeks. "And there's much more from where that came."

I didn't even try to question him about that. I knew that he was certain about what he just prophesized.

He then lifted my legs and shoved them over his shoulders. My pussy was lined up to his dick and I just noticed that a bead of pre-cum was coming out through the little slit.

For a moment, nothing happened. Leonardo was just taking in what his eyes were seeing.

Even though it was dark, his eyes behaved like they were from a cat. He could see all the curves, the wetness coming from my womb, and the way my pussy folds pulsed.

"God, you are so perfect..." He murmured, sliding his dick right inside my pussy, and he met no resistance other than my hymen. When the head of his cock was pressing against it, he thrust his hips forward slightly, popping it. It happened in a fraction of a second. I didn't even have time to notice what was happening before it was too late.

"Should I go all the way in? They want me to do that?" He murmured into my ear, nibbling on my earlobe.

I didn't even know if that was a real question or not. I just nodded. It was basically the only thing that could be done.

Then, seconds later, he started to roll his hips slowly. His pace was excruciatingly slow in the beginning, taking his time. What he promised before was coming to fruition. He was doing this so slowly I knew it was going to take me a lot of time until I hit my orgasm.

CHAPTER 5

And it happened. That same night, he took my virginity, and… then never showed up again. I was still on the ship, fighting against the motion sickness that came with it. I looked through the whole structure for Leonardo, but couldn't find him. I had no idea where he went or what his intentions were, but it was obvious that he wanted me just for that one-night stand and that was it.

I was so pissed off that, when I received a letter weeks after that, I wanted to tear it. I wanted to tear it until it was nothing more than hundreds of pieces.

I was gripping the letter so hard my knuckles were going white. I flipped the letter in my hands again and again, hoping that I was going to catch the name of the person who was playing this joke on me. I mean, we didn't dock anywhere, didn't stop for anything at any port, and we had phones and everything we needed to keep in contact with the people we loved.

It was for that reason that I didn't even want to open the letter, even though I was tempted to do so. I sat on the bed, barely aware of my dress. It was a tight fit. It fit nicely around my body, highlighting my curves. I knew that because Sofia said that I looked good. Considering that she hated me, that compliment meant a lot.

My fingers were shaking, but it was okay. I then pried open the letter slowly, fishing out of it a small piece of paper. It was ripped. The sides were ripped, as if someone did whatever was behind this hastily.

"Whoever is playing this joke on me is going to pay for it," I muttered, shooting up when I realized that I recognized that handwriting. I thought he wasn't going to come. I thought he wasn't on the ship, but now he wanted to meet up with me? This whole time, avoiding me even though I always went everywhere on the ship, always trying to make new friends and get to know new people?

I had no idea what was going on in his mind, but I had to make a decision.

I was pondering what decision I was going to make when I remembered that soon we were going to be docking at our final destination. Once we were there, I wouldn't be able to continue living in this dream.

Leonardo took my virginity, made me feel impossibly good, and I wanted more of that. I had no idea if he somehow fell off the ship, but even if that happened, I could have whatever I wanted with another man.

Gervasio also started to avoid me. I wondered what was up with that.

I crumpled the piece of paper and the cover of the letter with my right hand, tossing the ball into the trash bin. Standing up, I started to make my way toward where the piece of paper said I should meet up with Girolamo. He said he was going to be there, and I had a million questions to ask him. None of them were going to be easy, but they had to be made anyway.

I crossed several hallways, rooms, and whatever else the ship had until I got to the other end of it. I was in a place where I could see the ocean and some blocks of ice floating on it. It was cold, but not too much. Not to mention that I was still inside the ship. It was just that, from where I was, I could see everything thanks to the glass panels that replaced what were supposed to be walls.

I put my hands on my waist as I turned my head left and right, pouting. I was already getting furious at the fact that he wasn't here. Girolamo said that he was going to be here, and he was never someone that didn't do good on his promises.

While I was in my high heels, I murmured, "Where the fuck

are you?"

Moments later, when I thought that he really wasn't going to show up and that this was nothing more than a ruse, I turned around as I felt a hand settling on my shoulder.

I flinched for a moment. The last thing I thought was going to happen was someone putting a hand on my shoulder.

Fisting my hand, I was ready to punch his face until he was begging for mercy when I realized that he was none other than Girolamo himself. It had been such a long time since the last time I met him, and I was shocked at how much he changed over the years.

He looked exuberant, handsome, and excessively sexy.

He had a dark suit on with a red tie, making him look even hotter than he was. He was my college crush, from the time when I thought I knew about everything in the world. His beard was made, looked sharp, and his hair cut short and licked to the side.

His eyes were dark green, regarding me with impossible curiosity. He was much taller than me, and it was as if he grew even taller than when we were 19. His presence was unmatched. Not even the guys that I met on the ship were like him in that regard.

He retreated his hand slowly, letting his arm fall to the side of his body.

"Miriam, you came. I thought you weren't going to. I know about everything that happened while you were on the ship. I just showed up here, but I've been following you. They want to kill you."

I took a step backward, not knowing if I should feel more lust for him or if I should be scared of him. What he just said was out of this world. People wanted to murder me? Who?

I didn't know if I believed him, but the determination in his eyes showed me that he wasn't kidding when he said that.

"What do you mean?" I asked, stepping farther away from him because it was the only thing I could do right now. It wasn't just his appearance that was different, but also the way with which he carried himself. It was almost as if he was an assassin.

"It means that I came here for you, and there's no time to

explain why," he said, marching toward me and cornering me against a wall. I felt my butt bumping against it and I realized that I could go no further.

He planted both of his hands against the wall behind me. Then, lowering his head, I didn't try to stop him when his lips touched mine. An electrical shock traversed my body, making me feel waves of pleasure and lust.

When I said I wanted to continue making my dream a reality on the ship, I didn't think that things were going to happen so quickly and suddenly. His lips were soft, sweet, and also incredibly wet, which was just the way I liked them.

It was as if our kiss went on for hours, even though it couldn't have been more than seconds, I thought when he retreated his head, blinking once and slowly.

I could only wonder what was going on in his head right now.

"What the hell was that?" I asked, noticing that he wasn't moving away. If anything, he was standing right where he was, his eyes gazing into mine.

"I'm going to save you, that's what's going to happen. I'm going to take you away from here."

"But how?" I asked when he kissed me again, his lips rubbing vigorously against mine, wetting them and turning me into stone, or almost. I couldn't move my body, melting in what he was doing to me.

I had difficulty breathing. I thought I was going to die suffocated, but then he pulled away without warning. When I reopened my eyes, I noticed that he was already taking off the coat of his suit. He tossed it to the side and then his hands went to where the buttons of his shirt were. As he undid one of them after the other, I knew what was going to happen and I wanted every second of it.

He was going to have sex with me as well. I didn't think it possible, that three hot men were going to fuck me while I was on the ship.

His eyes went up and down, taking in what they were seeing.

"And given that they can't know where you are right now, I'm going to fuck you. It's what I've always been thinking about ever since we graduated from college."

"What?" I squeaked, but it wasn't like he was even thinking about answering that. One moment he was standing where he was and then, the next, he was butt-naked. I knew he worked out, and that his body was built like a tank, but I didn't think that he was so good-looking.

We didn't have the same age gap that I had with the other guys, but it wasn't like the age difference mattered so much right now.

All I knew was that his cock was big and that I wanted to be all over it.

When he noticed the wicked smile on my face, he said, "I knew you were going to change your mind about it so soon."

"I'm beginning to think that you aren't so different from those other guys…"

I went to my knees right away, taking in what my eyes were seeing. It was his shaft, standing probably in front of me, making me drool and lick my lips.

I lifted my hand slowly, carefully wrapping my fingers around the circumference of his shaft. It was hot, blood pulsing in his veins. I tugged at the skin slowly and then wrapped my lips around his mushroom-like cockhead, loving the feel of it against them.

It was a mouthful. His cockhead was just so big that it stretched my lips beyond any level I thought possible. I swirled my tongue around it, and then one more time, and then one other time, until I felt like I couldn't have enough of it.

His balls were unattended and I couldn't let that be. Realizing that, I cupped them with my hand, playing with his balls. Even though things just barely started, I knew that he was already on the verge of having his climax. So much so that I started to slow things down. I didn't want this to end so quickly.

His balls were heavy and laden with his milk. I knew that because they were also lovingly warm. So warm that it was impossible for me not to be playing with them for what felt like hours. In the meantime, I kept bobbing up and down on his cock, feeling every inch of it. Well, not every inch of it because I didn't want to start to gag.

I wasn't going to deep-throat this man. If I did that, it would be like committing suicide.

He put his hand on my head, dictating the pace he wanted. I just kept on doing what I was doing, tasting his pre-come. As the seconds passed and I realized that our fun was ending, I decided to speed up things.

Moments later, he exploded inside my mouth. Rope after rope of his come, he shot his milk inside of it, allowing me to taste its salty flavor. It was intoxicating and almost like a drug. I couldn't have enough of it and I was pretty sure that I was going to be dependent on it.

When I pulled my head back even though I didn't want to, I noticed that my lips were coated with his come. What he was seeing made him smile.

And then, after putting his clothes on, he grabbed my arm and announced, "Come on. We're leaving now."

CHAPTER 6

I could do nothing to stop him as he put me in the helicopter and then we took off toward the coast. It was relatively close. So much so that I was able to see it from the helicopter the moment that we were hovering over the ship. For the next few minutes, I was already on the coast, in a hotel, and forgotten about. I was forgotten by Girolamo and I didn't even know where he went.

I knew that it was a mistake what he did. He shouldn't have left me alone. What if the other guys came here for me? They had their chance to kill me when we were alone and squandered it. I was pretty sure that they were coming for me.

It was for that reason that I looked outside the window of the tiny apartment where I was. It was dark outside, the moon high in the sky and the clouds around it. Everything was quiet around me and I could even hear the slow beatings of my heart.

I sighed, turning around slowly when I realized that I could finally hear something weird. For a moment, I thought that it was coming from down below, from the street, but then I realized that it was actually coming from the sky.

I just looked up and noticed that it was a helicopter, piloted by a man. It took me a while to notice it, but I soon figured out that the pilot was none other than Gervasio himself! The man that was supposed to become my husband was coming for me, and the glare in his eyes told me that he didn't like that I'd fled.

I flustered, pacing around the room and cooking up a plan. I had to leave the room somehow if I wanted to avoid them coming in here and getting to me. If that happened, I didn't know what would then ensue. They'd surely kill me. Even though I thought several times a day that living wasn't worth it, the last thing I wanted right now was to die.

I was just thinking that I was going to leap into the elevator and then out of here when the door slammed open. I let out a little scream, noticing that one of the men that did that was none other than Leonardo himself.

He had a gun with him that was tucked in his waist and it had a silencer. I didn't want to think about what he was going to do with it. He was probably going to kill me.

I was in the kitchen and so my hand snatched a knife. I held it in front of me while pointing it at them. Leonardo held up his hands, but the wicked smile on his face told me that he wasn't afraid of me.

"What do you think you're doing now, princess?" He asked, stepping toward me and then wrapping his fingers around my wrist. I didn't try cutting him with the knife. The power that he held over me was nothing short of incredible, and I knew that I was supposed to do everything he wanted.

"You came here to finish the job," I accused, lowering my eyes.

He planted his hand on my chin, lifting it. "Who said that? Frankly, I'm disappointed that you just up and left in that helicopter. Who did that with you?"

"I'm not going to answer that. I don't want to put his life at risk..." I responded.

"You already are by not telling us the truth," he said, squeezing my wrist slightly so that I dropped the knife. A short, brief clink echoed in the room and then he took me to the kitchen island, where he made me sit on it.

He lowered his head, moving it around my neck and shoulders.

He sniffed me, closing his eyes slowly while Gervasio stepped toward us and then started to play with my breast.

"We are actually fighting for you. When this is over, you'll have to tell us what you really think about us, who you prefer," he murmured, finally making something in my mind click.

This was why this was all happening. They were fighting for my love, which was something that flattered me.

Suddenly, I also realized that if they really wanted to kill me now, they'd already have done so.

And so, I had no choice but to fall into their embrace of me, my nightie suddenly being pulled up, and there was nothing that I could do about that. Gervasio was then all over my boob, mauling on it and loving my nipple with his tongue. When I looked down, he even met my eyes, telling me a million things through them.

Then, his hand found my thigh, going up and encountering my little snatch. He skipped my clit and went straight for the honey pot, slipping a finger inside of it. He moaned and then murmured something that I couldn't make out, even though I was pretty sure that it had something to do with the fact that he was in love with me. Or just with my boobs. Regardless, it was hot and it was making it difficult for me to breathe.

Leonardo, in the meantime, wasted no time before finding himself between my legs. He put both of his hands on them, moving them aside slowly. He widened the gap between my legs and then lowered his head. When he put his tongue outside his mouth, I knew what he was going to do and I braced myself for it.

Gervasio crashed his lips against mine, putting his tongue inside my mouth moments later. We had a short tongue battle, and it didn't last much more than a couple seconds. It made sense that it didn't. I was nothing more than a little princess for him and I needed to keep that in mind.

Nevertheless, when he took hold of the kiss, I thought I was going to pass out. A moment later, I felt my body lying on the kitchen island, with both of the men standing on top of me. One was pleasing my cunt however he could and the other was doing unspeakable things to my pair of boobs.

"I don't know how you managed to stay virgin for so long until I took it," one of the guys said and I didn't even know who it was. All I knew was that one of these men was lapping up at my snatch, making my whole body shiver. In the meantime, the other was roaming his hands over my breasts, kneading and fumbling with them.

I thought I was going to climax and I wasn't surprised when it happened. All I knew was that my body started to shake violently over and over. I thought I was going to pass out and the only thing keeping me from doing that was the fact that I could feel both of these men on top of me.

"Wait!" I begged them, reopening my eyes before I noticed that a shadow was standing behind them. For a moment, I thought that it was a stranger, but then I realized that it was just Girolamo. The glare in his eyes was telling. He didn't like an ounce of what was happening and wanted revenge.

I thought about sitting up and begging him not to do anything, but then I realized that he was curling up the side of his lips. I thought that that was weird, but then it lasted only a couple of seconds.

"Well, boys. I knew you were hungry for her, but I didn't think that you were *this* hungry."

He wasn't against them. Girolamo was actually with them, with Leonardo and Gervasio and I thought that such a thing was impossible.

He waved his hands and they both went to the side, making space for him. A second later, he was the one between my legs. He grabbed my thighs and started to knead the skin with his hands. They moved excruciatingly slowly, feeling the smoothness and softness of it.

"I went out for only a couple of minutes and you are already in deep trouble with them," he murmured, lowering his body as I figured out what he was going to do.

With his tongue out, he started to lap up at my pussy, making me arch my back. My cunt was so wet I knew it was never going to be like that again in my life. Girolamo was relentless, sometimes licking at it quickly, other times slowing things down.

When he realized that I was already far too exhausted to continue, he grabbed me, turned me around gently on the kitchen island, pulled me down slightly until my feet were touching the floor, and then slid his dick right inside my cunt. I felt it going all the way until he was touching the end of my tunnel.

"I'm a little disappointed. I still have some inches left," he murmured, rolling his hips soon after. I started to moan and groan, matching him thrust for thrust. I was wild and realized that he was just the first man. The other guys were going to pound in and out of me as well, and it was going to be jaw-dropping.

He picked up his pace and I soon started to come, my body rocking back and forth over the kitchen island. I bit my bottom lip so hard I drew blood out, and that wasn't even the tip of the iceberg of my climax. I was panting, more exhausted than I was before, and feeling so dirty. And it wasn't just that, too. I felt more than dirty. I felt filthy.

Moments later, he pulled out. He did that so slowly I thought I was going to fight back to keep him inside of me for as long as possible, but I didn't. The reason behind that was also a very simple one. I looked up and then to the sides, seeing that the other guys were already coming where I was. One of them grabbed my thighs, pulled me toward him gently, and then eased his prick inside my womb.

I could feel his hands all over my body as he started to rock his hips forward and backward. Differently from Girolamo, he was relentless from the get-go, his balls slapping against my ass. Slapping sounds started to fill the room, blocking out everything that was happening around me.

And then, he came inside of me, filling me with rope after rope of his viscous sperm. It was warm, thick, and creamy. When he pulled out, a line of milk lingered between the slit of his mushroom cockhead and the entrance of my pussy, and it was so hot.

It split moments later, announcing that it was time for the last guy to have me. And he did that. He was already all the way inside of me even though he still had some inches left. I was disappointed that I couldn't have all of them inside of me, but I wasn't going to moan about that much.

All I knew was that I was already hitting another orgasm when he came inside of me too. They all did and, if they knocked me up, I wouldn't know who the father was, and that was… Okay. I wanted to be with all of them.

That was my final decision and nobody was going to change it.

The End

The next page has a teaser for the first book of the series. Go check it out! And lastly, leave your review. I love reading your feedback!

TEASER: CLAIMING HER AGE GAP

Series: First Time Quickies - 1

Seated on the couch, I had little idea about what I should be doing right now. I took sips from the wine I was holding in my hands and tried to look confident, even though doing so was like moving a mountain. It was so difficult to look confident when I was among several people so different from me.

They were all magnates, richer than I could ever imagine. My father was one of them, but he never gave me more money than he thought I was due. Not that I had a problem with that, just that it took away some of the freedom that I was supposed to have now that I was 21 years old.

21 years old and still a virgin, I lamented, trying not to think too hard about that. It was a topic that truly made me question the direction that my life took. I didn't want to think too hard about it, knowing that I would just start to question everything I did. If that happened, I was pretty sure that everything would get much worse.

I wore a flimsy, dark red dress that clung to my body, highlighting my curves. It felt a bit too tight, but it wasn't the tighter piece that I had in my wardrobe. I liked tight clothes and I wasn't going to hide that. So much so that I wasn't ashamed of the glances that I caught in my direction. Dirty, older men that should be more concerned about what their wives were doing given that they weren't at home now.

I was so much younger than them that I felt displaced, knowing that the hours were going to keep passing and I wasn't going to be able to talk to any of them. I knew that they wanted to talk, but I was also aware that they just wanted to take me to their bedroom, where they could do whatever they wanted to me.

As if to show me that I was wrong about my assumptions, my eyes caught sight of a shadow that I should have overlooked. And it wasn't even just a normal, mundane shadow, but a man unlike the rest in the room. The moment my eyes were on him, I knew he was different and younger than everyone else in the room, but also much older than me.

He held a wine glass in his hand as well, but something about the way he was doing that told me that he had a level of self-esteem unmatched. He knew his place in the world, where he stood among all the men in the room, and that he had come here for someone specific.

Thinking back to what my father had said, I knew that that person was none other than me. To save our family, he sold me for his business. I was supposed to marry a Mafia boss, which was ridiculous. Who in their right mind would agree to something like that? I didn't know, but I had to take the dive anyway. There had been no other choice.

It was my chance to get out from under my father's scrutiny, which was something I had been wanting since I turned 15. My father was always worried about me, concerned that I was doing something wrong, always keeping me on a tight leash. I found it difficult just to breathe. And the worst thing was that I couldn't even go and see my friends, other than when I had classes.

I had no idea, nevertheless, if that sexy and hot man on the other side of the room was even interested in me. I had no idea if he truly was one of the Mafia bosses that came here just for me. It could be very well that he was here for someone else that didn't have anything to do with me.

I sighed, taking another sip of the wine, noticing that now it was too hot. I didn't even like wines that much. I was only drinking the red wine in the wine glass because I wanted to look the part, even though now I knew that doing so was impossible. I was pretty much the only woman at the party, after all. All I could see were men and other men, chatting among themselves as if they owned the world.

The man that was on the other side of the room was nothing short of perfect, probably standing over six foot five tall, his dark suit doing very little in terms of hiding his muscles. They flexed and strained against the material, making me wonder what he looked like without it on. I didn't know anything about the guy yet, but I'd definitely let him take my V-card, if he wanted it.

I could close my eyes and imagine him on top of me, peppering me with passionate kisses that would send me through the roof. I imagined his hot body grinding against mine, making me feel small and insignificant. Was that such an impossible thing to ask for? I didn't think so, which was why, in case he was my promised one, I wondered if I had a good chance of making that happen.

I put the glass with wine back down on the table by my side, saying to myself that I didn't want it anymore. But the real reason why I did that was that I was paralyzed. The man who I thought would never have eyes for me just glanced in my direction and held my gaze.

He was staring at me as if he knew I was his promised one. I couldn't even blink, knowing that he was a man assured of himself who was used to getting everything his way.

MORE BOOKS LIKE THIS ONE

SERIES - ONE WOMAN MANY MEN

1. Filling Her Rear: Aggressive Brat Sharing on New Year's Eve
2. Filling Her Rear: Aggressive BBW Backdoor Domination

3. Losing Control: Extreme Backdoor Ganging

4. Looting the Backdoor: A Ganging First Time Story

SERIES - IN PUBLIC

1. Fed from Behind: Rear Entrance Devoured by Multiple Men
2. Fed from Behind: Tight Squeeze by Multiple Men
3. Fed from Behind: Taken by Multiple Men on Christmas Day
4. Fed from Behind: Tight Squeeze in front of the Christmas Tree
5. Tight Squeeze: Petite for Big Alpha Men of the House

ABOUT THE AUTHOR

Leandra Camilli's obsession? Writing dirty, steamy stories that make her readers drool. She loves her Alpha males, hucows, sissies, and futas. If you're looking for those kinds of books, look no further.

With a cup of coffee on her table and warm socks on, she writes almost every day. Leandra Camilli has featured in several top 100 categories in the store, and she publishes weekly. Check her mailing list to download two free stories (one about an overly naughty hucow, and the second featuring a younger man claiming his best friend's MILF). You can also find her Facebook page below.